Snuffy's Favorite Color

Adapted by Kelli Chipponeri
Based on a teleplay by John Semper, Jr.

PSS!
PRICE STERN SLOAN

Characters created by David and Deborah Michel.

© 2002 Jay Jay the Jet Plane Productions, Inc. and KidQuest, Inc. d/b/a WonderWings.com
Entertainment. All Rights Reserved. Jay Jay The Jet Plane, Jay Jay, Snuffy, Brenda Blue, Tarrytown Airport,
and Smiling Meadow are trademarks of KidQuest, Inc. d/b/a WonderWings.com Entertainment.
Published by Price Stern Sloan, a division of Penguin Putnam Books for Young Readers, 345 Hudson
Street, New York, NY 10014. PSS! is a registered trademark of Penguin Putnam Inc. Printed in U.S.A.

ISBN 0-8431-4903-5   C D E F G H I J

Concert Day at Tarrytown had been a big success. Everyone sang a song about his or her favorite color. But Snuffy couldn't decide what his favorite color was, so he sang a song about *all* the colors!

"Concert Day was supersonic!" said Jay Jay as he flew up next to Snuffy. "Your rainbow song was the best part of the show! You must be feeling pretty good."

"I am," said Snuffy. "But everyone else picked a favorite color to sing about, and I couldn't figure out my favorite color. Choosing a favorite color is one of the hardest things I have ever tried to do."

"Hey, Snuffy," said Jay Jay. "I have an idea. When I have trouble figuring something out, I go see Brenda Blue."

"That's a great idea! Thanks, Jay Jay," called Snuffy. He headed toward Tarrytown Airport and Brenda Blue's workshop.

When Snuffy arrived at the workshop, he found Brenda Blue working on a small motor. "Hi, Brenda," said Snuffy. "Hi, Snuffy. What's wrong?" asked Brenda.

"I can't decide on a favorite color," said Snuffy.

"Well, it seems to me if something is your favorite, you probably see it a lot. Right?" asked Brenda.

"Yes," said Snuffy. "I would probably see it every day!"

"And if something is your favorite, you probably like it a lot, too. Right?" asked Brenda.

"Yes," said Snuffy. "If it's my favorite, I'd really love it."

"So you should figure out your favorite color based on the things you see today," explained Brenda. "And pay special attention to what you love the most."

"What a super idea! Thanks, Brenda!" exclaimed Snuffy as he flew up into the sky.

Snuffy was ready to put his plan into action, so he looked at the things around him. "Hmmm, the sun above me is yellow. Maybe yellow should be my favorite color," he said. "But my skywriting smoke is white and so are the clouds, so maybe white should be my favorite color."

"Hey, Snuffy!" called Jay Jay. "How's it going?"
"I'm still trying to choose my favorite color," replied Snuffy.
"Want to join me for some crop watering?" asked Jay Jay.
"That would be great!" answered Snuffy.
"Let's go fill up our water tanks," suggested Jay Jay.

"There you go, guys!" said Brenda Blue. "Your water tanks are filled to the brim."

"Thanks, Brenda!" cheered Jay Jay. "I don't know what we would do without you."

"You're the best," agreed Snuffy.

"Come on, Snuffy. We have work to do," said Jay Jay, and they taxied down the runway.

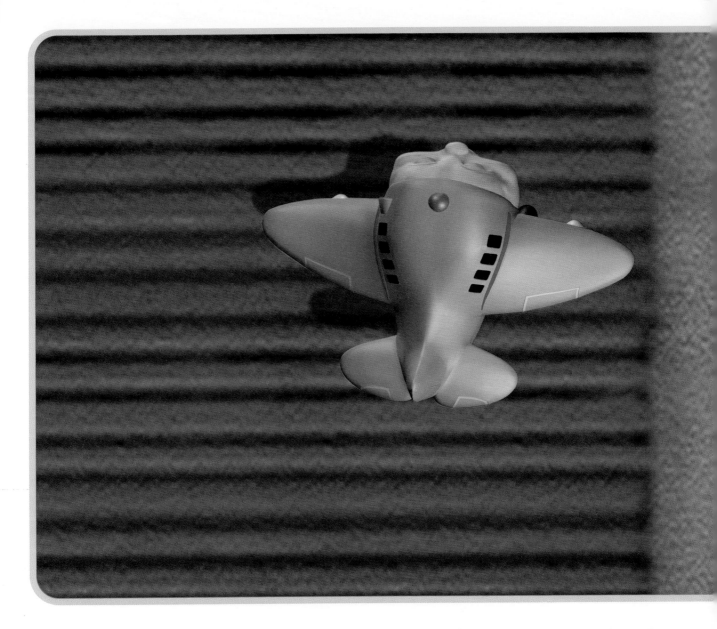

Jay Jay and Snuffy arrived at Farmer Dale's field. As they sprayed water on the crops, Snuffy was thinking about what his favorite color might be.

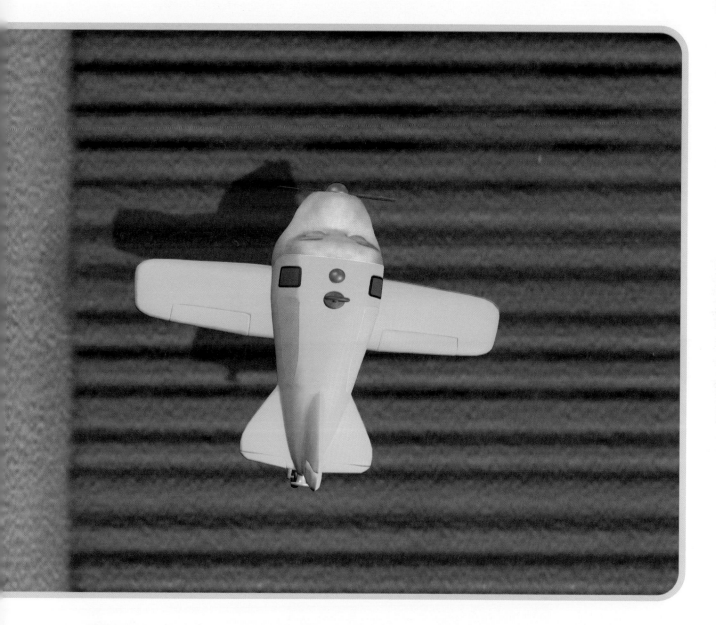

"Hmmm, parts of the field are brown, so maybe brown should be my favorite color."

"And the corn stalks are green. Maybe green should be my favorite color. But when the corn is picked, it is yellow, just like the sun. That's two votes for yellow, so maybe that should be my favorite color."

"Okay, Snuffy," said Jay Jay. "We have a lot of deliveries to make. We had better head back to Tarrytown Airport to refuel."

**Back at Tarrytown Airport, Brenda Blue filled up their gas tanks.
"You guys are refueled and ready to make your deliveries," she said.**

"Thanks, Brenda!" called Jay Jay and Snuffy as they left the airport.
"Boy, that Brenda Blue sure is a big help," said Snuffy.
"No kidding," agreed Jay Jay. "She takes good care of us."

While he was flying, Snuffy thought to himself, "I love making deliveries. So what colors do I see when I make them? That big barn near the river is red. Maybe red should be my favorite color."

"And the flowers of Smiling Meadow are purple and orange. Maybe one of those should be my favorite color," said Snuffy.

Their deliveries took them over the docks of Tarrytown. Snuffy looked again for a favorite color. "Wow!" exclaimed Snuffy. "Look at those boats. One is pink, one is black, and another is gold. Maybe one of those colors is my favorite."

"What are you thinking about, Snuffy?" asked Jay Jay.

"I am still trying to figure out what my favorite color is," said Snuffy.

"Well, maybe you will get lucky and it will come to you," said Jay Jay.

"Like a flash of lightning.."

Just then, there was a flash of light and a rumbling sound in the sky. "That doesn't sound good," said Jay Jay.

The sky filled with clouds, and rain began to fall. "We better go home," said Snuffy.

As Snuffy and Jay Jay flew back to Tarrytown Airport, they got all wet, but they knew when they arrived, Brenda Blue would be waiting with a dry towel.

"How are you feeling, Snuffy?" asked Brenda as she finished drying him off.

"I feel great," replied Snuffy. "Thanks."

"Good. I wouldn't want you to get rusty," she said. "Okay, Jay Jay. It's your turn."

Snuffy moved to the hangar door and noticed a rainbow. He remembered he hadn't picked a favorite color. "Brenda said I should think of something I love and that might help me choose. And Brenda's always right," thought Snuffy. "In fact, Brenda is one of the most helpful people ever."

"She fills our water tanks when they are empty, she refuels us when we are out of gas, she dries us off when we get wet, and much more. I sure do love Brenda a lot," said Snuffy.

"Hey, that's it!" exclaimed Snuffy.
"What's it?" asked Brenda Blue.
"I just figured out my favorite color!" exclaimed Snuffy.

"That's great, Snuffy," said Jay Jay. "What is it?"
"Not what," said Snuffy. *"Who!"*
"Who?" asked Brenda and Jay Jay, looking confused.

"Blue!" replied Snuffy. "Brenda Blue!"

"Me, Snuffy?" asked Brenda Blue. "Why am I your favorite color?"

"I get it," said Jay Jay. "He sees you every day, he loves you a lot, and without you, none of the things he does would be possible."

"Aw, that's so sweet, Snuffy," said Brenda Blue.
"Gee whiz, Brenda," said Snuffy, smiling sheepishly.

So, Snuffy finally found his favorite color—blue!